A Dirty Story

By Sarah Brennan

Illustrated by

Harry Harrison

perfect pixels & print

Publisher:

Angels On Pins

Lake Cottage, Beccles Road,
Fritton, Great Yarmouth,
Norfolk, England
Tel: +44 1493 488 320
Fax: +44 1493 488 297

In association with

PPP Company Ltd
20/F, 75-77 Wyndham Street,
Central, Hong Kong
Tel: +852 2973 6791
Fax: +852 2869 4554
E-mail: ppp@ppp.com.hk
URL: www.ppp.com.hk

ISBN 962-86877-8-6

Printed by Sunland Printing Ltd

For all children, be they Neats or Grots,
and especially for
Beatrice and Annabel (SB),
Charlie and Lucy (HH).

4

This is a story for girls and boys
Who don't like putting away their toys;
Who think a bed is a trampoline
And can't be bothered to keep things clean.

Yes, this is a story for all those kids
Who leave on taps but who leave off lids
(It's also a story for mums and dads
To stop them going completely mad...).

It all begins on a tidy street
The pride and joy of a town called Neat;
The sort of street which ensures the fame
Of towns with such an unusual name.

The street had houses down either side
Which weren't too thin and which weren't too wide,
As bright as buttons and all the same
Like houses in a Monopoly game.

At Number One there was Mrs Green
Who never smiled till her house was clean,
And Mr Purple at Number Two
Was always looking for chores to do.

Old Miss Yellow at Number Three
Polished the floors from lunch till tea.
The Orange family at Number Four
Scrubbed so hard that their hands got sore.

Number Five housed Grandpa Red
Who pottered for hours in his garden shed,
And all the Browns at Number Six
Loved to hammer and saw and fix.

At Number Seven the young Miss Pink
Spent all day by the kitchen sink
(Which some would say had a lot to do
With Number Eight's dashing Mr Blue).

Mrs White kept her washing line
Draped with nappies at Number Nine
And last of all there was Number Ten,
Grey's Apartment for Gentlemen.

And all these houses I've talked about
Were clean as whistles inside and out.

Their windows glistened, their doorknobs shone,
Their polished floors could be eaten on,
Their beds were made at the crack of dawn
And toys were never left on the lawn.

Their garden beds were a picture too,
Where daisies, poppies and sunflowers grew,
And all the borders were mown and green,
With not a dandelion to be seen.

8

And never in all the town of Neat
Was ever there such a tidy street.

9

Not far away lay another town,
A town of equally great renown:-
Renown for everything Neat was not
And so it went by the name of Grot.

The town of Grot, like the town of Neat,
Took great delight in a certain street:-
The vilest street you could ever know
Where tidy people would never go.

The road was crooked and cracked and rough
And cluttered up with revolting stuff,
Like broken bottles and bones of cats
And dead canaries and poisoned rats.

The people lived in a ghastly mess,
They never bothered to change their dress,
Their hair was scruffy and full of fleas
And all the children had dirty knees.

They never polished their window panes,
They left the washing up till it rained.
They never weeded a garden bed
And in the gutters, mosquitoes bred.

And never in all the town of Grot
Was ever there such a grotty spot!

Now Neat and Grot were the largest towns
In the famous district of Twinkle Downs,
Which every year would award a star
To the cleanest town in the area.

Now some of you have already guessed
The town the judges declared was best.
Yes, year by year, it was always Neat,
And all because of its tidy street.

And some of you will already know
That seeds of envy quickly grow
When someone's winning an awful lot
And every other contestant's not.

And so, one year, when the contest came,
The Grots decided to spoil the game.
(The Grots may not have been very neat
But every Grot was an expert cheat.)

12

The Neats were slaving from dawn till night
To make their town look exactly right,
And no one slackened or dragged their feet
Especially not in the tidy street.

Mr Purple and Mrs Green
Rubbed the floors to a lovely sheen.
Old Miss Yellow and Grandpa Red
Tidied everyone's garden bed.

The Oranges went on scrubbing sprees,
The Browns pruned everybody's trees,
Young Miss Pink and Mr Blue
Snapped up all the jobs for two.

And Mrs White and all those Greys
Washed and ironed for days and days.
And never had all the townsfolk seen
A street so beautifully neat and clean.

13

The evening prior to judging day
The Neats put all of their tools away.
They went to bed and they closed their eyes
And dreamed of winning the famous prize.

The night grew dark and the Neats slept sound,
The moon rose, golden and fat and round,
Then suddenly, with a dreadful din,
A pack of horrible Grots raced in!

They clogged the gutters and blocked the drains,
They squirted mud on the window panes.
They smeared the walls with their filthy paws
And threw tomatoes at all the doors.

They trampled flowers and jumped on trees,
They filled the gardens with flies and fleas.
They fouled the road with a sickly slime
And all in all had a lovely time.

And never in all the town of Neat
Was there ever such an untidy street!

15

The Grots ran off as the first cock crowed
And hurried home to their filthy road.
The Neats woke up in a few hours more
And just imagine the sight they saw!

They gnashed their teeth and they wept and wailed,
They vowed to have the intruders jailed.
They called the police and the army too
But there was nothing that they could do.

They phoned the Council of Twinkle Downs
But all the judges were on their rounds.
It seemed as clear as the morning skies
Another township would win the prize.

(The Grots were sly as a Grot could be
And sent a message of sympathy.)

17

Now all the judges of Twinkle Downs
Were, as I've said, on their annual rounds.

They drove about in a little van
With Council paper and pen in hand.
They nudged and muttered and wrote things down
In every street and in every town.

They passed through Grimy and Not-so-Hot,
They zoomed as fast as they could through Grot,
They checked on Average and Just-So-So
And then there was only Neat to go.

Now contest judging is quite a chore
And even judges get tired and sore
So, just before they arrived in Neat,
They took a break for a bite to eat.

And as they munched on their hot meat pies
A dreadful thunder cloud met their eyes!
The cloud was making horrendous sounds
And billowing over Twinkle Downs!

19

It swept along till it came to Neat
And stopped just over its famous street.
The judges jumped in their little van
And, seconds later, the storm began.

It cleared the gutters and cleaned the drains,
It rinsed the mud from the windowpanes.
It washed the paw marks from all the walls
And lashed tomato seeds off the doors.

It bathed the flowers and it lifted trees,
It drove away all the flies and fleas.
As tough as Grots, but in half the time,
The storm got rid of their grotty grime.

The dirt and litter and mud and stains
All poured away down the local drains.
They joined the river in one foul lot
And flooded down to the town of Grot.

And all the people of Grot got stuck
From top to toe in their ghastly muck!

The storm cloud lifted, the sun shone bright,
The town of Neat was a wondrous sight.
The tidy street was its pride once more
And twice as clean as it was before!

The judges, brimming with hot meat pies,
Inspected it with their practised eyes.
So neat it was, they were moved to say
"The finest street we have seen today!"

They kindly smiled at the weary Neats
"We like your houses, we like your streets,
Your tidy town is the best by far
So once again we give you the Star!"

Now I'm quite sure you will understand
Why some might say that the storm was planned.
For suddenly, out of the damp and heat,
There rose a miracle in the street!

Yes, from its houses a rainbow grew
In every glorious rainbow hue
Until it covered the tidy town
And lingered there till the sun went down.

So now we've come to the final scene,
You'll know it pays to be neat and clean.
You'll also know what a silly clot
A kid would be to become a Grot.